Time's Revolution

Take Control of Your Time to Transform Your Life

Deepak Singh

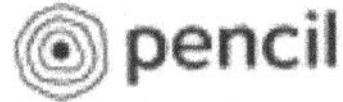
pencil

ISBN 978-93-5667-745-6
© Deepak Singh 2023

Published in India 2023 by Pencil

A brand of
One Point Six Technologies Pvt. Ltd.
Unit no. 26, Ground Floor, Building A1,
Wadala Truck Terminal Road,
Near Post Office, Antop Hill, Mumbai - 400037
E connect@thepencilapp.com
W www.thepencilapp.com

DISCLAIMER: *The opinions expressed in this book are those of the authors and do not purport to reflect the views of the Publisher.*

Author biography

Hello! I'm happy to meet you, I'm Deepak Singh. I work as a research analyst and am passionate about writing books and doing research on the planet Earth, space, and the art of living. I most likely have high analytical and critical thinking abilities that enable me to assess data, spot trends, and reach conclusions in my capacity as a research analyst. As part of my job, I might perform primary and secondary research, analyze available data, and provide findings to guide individual, corporate, or organizational decision-making. I adore writing and researching as interests in space and Earth in my free time. You can tell that I have an open mind and am interested in learning about the world around me.

CONTENTS

Epigraph

"Time is not an adversary; how we use it defines our success."

Foreword

Time is a valuable commodity in today's fast-paced world. With so much to accomplish and so little time, it's easy to become worried and overwhelmed. As a result, good time management is more crucial than ever.

"Time's Revolution: Take Control of Your Time to Transform Your Life" is a must-read for everyone interested in learning how to successfully manage their time. This book will teach you practical ideas and techniques for making the most of your time and achieving your goals.

What I like about this book is that it doesn't just provide you a list of time management tips and tactics. Instead, it takes a comprehensive approach, assisting you in understanding the fundamental principles of time management and equipping you with the skills and methods you require to succeed.

As someone who has previously suffered with time management, I can speak to the effectiveness of the tactics and ideas provided in this book. I've been able to accomplish more in less time and lessen my stress levels by following the suggestions in this book.

"Time's Revolution" is the book for you if you want to take control of your time and achieve your goals. So, whether you're a busy professional, a student, or anyone who wants to maximize their time, I encourage you to read this book and begin your own time revolution.

Preface

Welcome to "Time's Revolution: Take Control of Your Time to Transform Your Life." This book is the culmination of years of time management research, testing, and personal experience. Our goal is to present you with a complete guide that will assist you in taking charge of your time, accomplishing your goals, and living a satisfying life.

This book will cover everything from basic time management ideas to practical tools and methods for effective time management. We'll also look at some of the frequent roadblocks to successful time management and offer advice on how to overcome them.

Our strategy is based on the conviction that efficient time management does not entail cramming as much as possible into every minute of every day. Instead, it is about recognizing your priorities, being deliberate about how you spend your time, and focusing on the things that are most important to you.

We wrote this book with a diverse audience in mind, including students, professionals, entrepreneurs, and anyone else who wants to make the most of their time. This book has something for everyone, whether you're struggling to find time to achieve your goals or simply want to become more productive and efficient.

So, whether you're new to time management or a seasoned pro, we encourage you to join us on this path of discovery and transformation. We hope that at the end of this book, you will be motivated to take charge of your time, achieve your goals, and live a more fulfilling life.

Acknowledgements

Writing a book is never a solo endeavor, and "Time's Revolution: Take Control of Your Time to Transform Your Life" is no exception. We would like to offer our heartfelt appreciation to the following individuals:

First and foremost, we want to express our gratitude to our families for their constant support during this effort. They gave us the encouragement, love, and patience we needed to finish this book.

We'd like to thank our colleagues and friends for their contributions, feedback, and inspiration. Your words of encouragement and support kept us going.

Finally, we'd like to express our appreciation to our readers for their interest in this work. We hope that the concepts and tactics offered in this book will assist you in gaining control of your time, achieving your objectives, and living a satisfying life.

Thank you to everyone who supported me for this book. This project would not have been possible without your help.

Introduction

Time is the most valuable resource we have, and successfully managing it is critical to attaining our objectives and having a satisfying life. In this book, we'll look at time management principles and present practical tools and ideas for making the most of your time.

Time is a finite resource, and once it's gone, it's gone forever. That is why it is critical to carefully manage our time so that we may make the most of the time we have and achieve our goals.

"Time's Revolution: Take Control of Your Time to Transform Your Life" is a thorough time management guide that will teach you how to manage your time effectively so that you can achieve your objectives and live a full life. This book will teach you practical ideas and techniques for making the most of your time and becoming more productive and effective.

This book is for you if you are a student, a professional, an entrepreneur, or anyone who wants to make the most of their time. We'll go over time management principles, practical tools and tactics, and advice on how to overcome the hurdles that can get in the way of efficient time management.

You will have a better grasp of how to manage your time successfully by the end of this book, allowing you to achieve your goals, minimize stress, and live a more rewarding life. So, let's get started on the time revolution!

Chapter 1 The Value of Time Management

In this chapter, we'll look at the benefits of excellent time management and how it may help you achieve your objectives, reduce stress, and improve your overall quality of life.

The practice of organizing and planning how to distribute time effectively and efficiently is known as time management. It is a critical talent that enables people to prioritize their tasks and achieve their goals within a specified timeframe. Time is a limited resource that must be used effectively in order to achieve success in both personal and professional life.

Time management is important in many facets of life, both personal and professional. Some of the most important reasons for time management are as follows:

- **Aids in the achievement of goals:**Time management assists in creating realistic goals and working towards them within a specific time frame. Individuals with proper time management may prioritize their duties, provide enough time for each activity, and accomplish them on time.

- **Boosts productivity:**Increased productivity is the result of effective time management. Individuals can focus on their work and accomplish it quickly by organizing tasks, setting deadlines, and minimizing distractions. This, in turn, aids in achieving more meaningful effects in less time.

- **Stress reduction:**Stress, worry, and burnout can result from poor time management. Individuals can lessen the pressure and stress associated with meeting deadlines and attaining goals by planning and organizing their actions.

- **Improves decision-making abilities:**Individuals with time management abilities must prioritize work, analyze situations, and make informed judgments. This aids in the development of critical thinking and decision-making skills, both of which are necessary in personal and professional life.

- **Enhances work-life balance:**Individuals can efficiently combine their personal and professional duties with excellent time management. This results in a better work-life balance, which boosts general well-being and quality of life.

- **Improves self-discipline:**Self-discipline and self-motivation are required for time management. Individuals can increase their self-discipline and establish a strong work ethic by sticking to a schedule and completing deadlines.

- **Increases time utilization:**Effective time management aids in making the best use of available time. Individuals can make better use of their time and produce more meaningful achievements in less time by planning and prioritizing tasks.

Finally, time management is a vital ability that can lead to increased productivity, decreased stress, better decision-making abilities, and a better work-life balance. It is a skill that can be learned and honed over time, and it is necessary for personal and professional success.

Chapter 2 Setting Goals and Priorities

To properly manage your time, you must first choose what you want to do. In this chapter, we'll talk about how to develop objectives and priorities that correspond with your beliefs and life vision.

Goals and priorities must be established as part of personal and professional development. It is difficult to attain success in any aspect of life without defined goals and priorities. Goals offer the direction and purpose of our actions, whereas priorities help us focus on what is important and avoid wasting time on trivial chores. This chapter will discuss the significance of defining goals and priorities, as well as practical recommendations for effective goal setting.

Why establish goals and priorities?

Setting goals and priorities is essential for a variety of reasons. First and foremost, goals provide us with direction and purpose. They assist us in determining our goals and developing a strategy for achieving them. We may travel aimlessly through life without defined goals, unaware of what we want to accomplish or how to get there.

Second, goals allow us to track our progress and achievements. We can quickly understand how far we have come and what we need to do to achieve our intended outcome when we create specific, measurable goals. This can be quite motivating because it provides us with a sense of accomplishment and growth.

Third, priorities assist us in focusing on what is most essential. There are several demands on our time and attention in today's fast-paced society. It is easy to become distracted by irrelevant tasks and waste time on activities that do not contribute to our goals if we do not have clear priorities.

Effective Goal-Setting Techniques

- **Begin with the end in mind:**When defining goals, it is critical to first visualize the intended outcome. What do you hope to accomplish? What does success entail? Starting with the final goal in mind allows you to establish a clear picture of what you want to achieve, which will guide your actions and decisions.

- **Make your objectives explicit and quantifiable:**Goals should be detailed and measurable, with deadlines and milestones clearly defined. Instead of creating a goal to "exercise more," make a goal to "exercise for 30 minutes, three times per week, for the next six months." This goal is definite, quantifiable, and has a timetable for completion.

- **Goals should be prioritized:**Not all goals are created equal. Some objectives are more vital than others, and they must be prioritized accordingly. Consider which goals will have the greatest impact on your life or career, and prioritize them.

- **Divide your ambitions into tiny steps:**Large goals can be overwhelming, so breaking them down into smaller, more attainable tasks might help. This can help you keep track of your progress and prevent getting discouraged or overwhelmed.

- **Goals should be reviewed and adjusted on a frequent basis:**Goals are not fixed in stone, and they must be reviewed and adjusted on a regular basis. As circumstances change and new opportunities emerge, goals and timetables may need to be revised. Regular evaluations can assist in ensuring that goals stay relevant and attainable.

Conclusion

Goals and priorities must be established as part of personal and professional development. We may give direction and purpose to our actions, assess progress and track achievement, and focus our energies on what is truly important by defining clear, explicit goals and prioritizing them properly. With these goal-setting ideas, you may start achieving your goals and living a more purposeful and satisfying life.

Chapter 3 Auditing and Analyzing Time

Before you can begin managing your time, you must first understand how you currently spend it. We'll lead you through a time audit and analysis in this chapter to help you find opportunities for improvement.

We have a limited amount of time in each day, week, month, and year. To reach our goals and be successful in our personal and professional lives, we must successfully manage our time. A time audit and analysis is one method for properly managing time.

A time audit is a method of keeping track of how we spend our time throughout the day. It entails keeping track of what we do and how long we spend doing it. A time audit is intended to uncover how we spend our time, where we waste time, and where we may be more productive.

To conduct a time audit, you must first create a log that records all of your activity. A spreadsheet or a notepad can be used to keep the log. The date, time, action, and duration should all be included in the log. Every activity, including work-related duties, personal tasks, and leisure activities, should be documented.

After a week or two of recording your activities, you can analyze the data to uncover patterns and trends. This data can help you make more educated judgments about how you spend your time and make changes to become more productive.

When analyzing the data, keep the following in mind:

- **Waste of Time:**Determine which activities occupy a considerable amount of your time but provide no value to your life. Excessive social media use, TV viewing, and internet browsing are all examples.

- **Activities that are productive:**Identify activities that will help you improve personally and professionally. Exercise, reading, and learning new abilities are among the examples.

- **The time of day:**Determine when you are most productive and when you are least productive. This information can assist you in better planning your day and tackling difficult chores during your most productive period.

- **Priorities:**Identify and prioritize the tasks that are most important to you. This allows you to devote your time and energy to the most critical tasks while avoiding spending time on less important ones.

- **Possibilities for Improvement:**Determine where you can enhance your time management abilities.

To avoid overcommitting yourself, you may need to delegate chores or learn to say no.

Finally, a time audit and analysis is an excellent technique to better manage your time. It assists you in determining how you spend your time, where you waste time, and where you may be more effective. You can make the most of your time and achieve your goals by making informed decisions based on the data you collect.

Chapter 4 Scheduling and Planning

Once you've determined your goals and priorities, you can begin planning and scheduling your time. In this chapter, we'll discuss how to create a schedule that works for you and keeps you focused and productive.

Time management is a critical skill for achieving personal and professional success. Planning and scheduling are important aspects of time management. In this chapter, we will look at the significance of planning and scheduling, as well as the procedures involved in developing a plan and strategies for effective scheduling.

The significance of planning and scheduling

Planning and scheduling are essential components of efficient time management because they assist individuals in establishing priorities, allocating resources, and optimizing their time. Setting precise goals and outlining the activities required to attain them is what planning entails. Scheduling entails allocating time and defining when each job in the plan will be done. Planning and scheduling work together to help people make the most of their time by ensuring that they are working on the most important activities and allocating enough time to finish them.

Individuals who plan and schedule effectively can:

- Prioritize tasks and activities based on their significance and urgency.

- Set attainable goals and deadlines for accomplishing tasks.

- Avoid procrastination and better manage your time.

- Reduce stress while increasing output.

- Make the most of your resources and waste as little time as possible.

- Improve your work-life balance.

The steps involved in making a plan

Creating a strategy entails a number of processes, each of which is essential to ensuring that the plan is complete, reasonable, and achievable. For efficient planning, the following actions are recommended:

- **Identify the steps:**Break the goal down into smaller, more doable stages to attain it. Determine the tasks that must be completed and the resources required to perform each activity.

- **Estimate time and resources:**Estimate the time and resources needed to execute each task. This will assist you in developing a realistic timeline for the entire project.

- **Define the goal:**Begin by outlining the exact aim you wish to attain. This could be a long-term goal like finishing a degree program or starting a business, or it could be a short-term goal like finishing a project or reaching a deadline.

- **Set deadlines:**Establish deadlines for each assignment and the entire project. Make certain that your deadlines are both realistic and attainable.

- **Monitor progress:**Monitor your progress on a frequent basis to verify that you are on pace to meet your objectives. Make changes as needed to keep on track.

- **Prioritize tasks:**Sort your jobs according to their priority and urgency. This will allow you to concentrate on the most critical activities and prioritize your time and resources.

Scheduling Techniques for Success

Scheduling entails allocating time and defining when each job in the plan will be done. The following ideas can assist you in efficiently scheduling your time:

-
  Schedule your most important tasks first: Schedule your most critical duties first thing in the morning, when you are most productive. This will allow you to concentrate on the most critical tasks and accomplish them on time.

- **Use a calendar:**Schedule your projects and activities with a calendar. A physical calendar or a digital calendar.

- **Allow for flexibility:**Allow for schedule flexibility to allow unexpected events or changes in priorities. Make room in your schedule for unexpected jobs or crises.

- **Avoid multitasking:**As much as possible, avoid multitasking. Instead, concentrate on one activity at a time and allow enough time to finish it before moving on to the next.

- **Break tasks into smaller chunks:**Divide huge jobs into smaller, more doable portions. This will keep you from feeling overwhelmed and will make it easier to plan your time wisely.

- **Take breaks:**To minimize burnout and retain productivity, take regular breaks. Schedule short rest and recharge breaks throughout the day.

Finally, successful time management necessitates meticulous planning and scheduling. Individuals can prioritize tasks, set reasonable goals, optimize their time, and achieve a better work-life balance by following the stages indicated above and using the techniques for successful scheduling. Planning and scheduling are important abilities that can help people minimize stress, boost productivity, and achieve personal and professional success. Anyone can improve these skills and make the most of their time with practice and persistence.

Chapter 5 Getting Rid of Procrastination

Procrastination is one of the most significant impediments to efficient time management. In this chapter, we'll look at why we procrastinate and offer practical ideas and tactics for breaking the habit.

When it comes to efficiently managing their time, many people battle procrastination. It is defined as the act of delaying or putting off chores that must be accomplished, which frequently results in emotions of tension, anxiety, and overload. However, with a few basic tactics and a little willpower, you can overcome procrastination and become more effective with your time.

- **Determine the source of your procrastination:**The first step in overcoming procrastination is determining the root cause of your procrastination. Is it because you dislike or find the task difficult? Do you find yourself easily sidetracked by other things? Or are you feeling overburdened by the amount of work you need to complete? Once you've determined the root problem, you can start working on a solution.

- **Divide jobs into smaller, more doable chunks:**One of the most common reasons people procrastinate is that they are overwhelmed by the magnitude of the task at hand. To get around this, divide the task into smaller, more manageable chunks. This will make the task seem less onerous and will allow you to make progress, even if it is only a small amount at a time.

- **Establish attainable goals and deadlines:**Setting attainable objectives and deadlines might aid in staying on track and avoiding procrastination. Make certain that your Objectives are explicit, quantifiable, realistic, relevant, and time-bound. Setting deadlines for oneself creates a sense of urgency and increases your likelihood of prioritizing your task.

- **Remove all distractions:**Distractions are a significant cause of procrastination. Remove as many distractions as possible to overcome this. This could be turning off your phone, dismissing superfluous computer tabs, or locating a quiet location where you can concentrate.

- **To keep focused, set a timer:**Using a timer is an excellent approach to maintaining attention and minimizing procrastination. Set a timer for a particular amount of time, such as 25 minutes, and focus solely on the task at hand. Take a short rest when the timer has finished before starting the next timer.

- **Reward yourself as follows:**Finally, give yourself a reward for finishing your duties. This might be as simple as taking a break, going for a stroll, or indulging in your favorite snack. You will feel more driven to accomplish chores and avoid procrastination in the future if you reward yourself.

To summarize, overcoming procrastination is an important aspect of time management. You may overcome procrastination and become more productive with your time by recognizing the main reason for your procrastination, dividing jobs into smaller pieces, creating achievable objectives and deadlines, minimizing distractions, using a timer to keep focused, and rewarding yourself. Remember that overcoming procrastination requires time and effort, but with practice, you may develop the habits required for success.

Chapter 6 Time-saving Techniques

There are numerous time-saving tactics available to help you make the most of your time. In this chapter, we'll cover a number of productivity strategies and techniques for getting more done in less time.

The pressures of modern life can make it feel as if there are never enough hours in the day to get everything done. We may, however, make the most of the time we have and boost our productivity by employing time-saving measures.

- **Prioritize Your Tasks:**Prioritizing your work is one of the most effective time-saving tactics. Make a list of everything you need to complete, and then prioritize the most vital tasks. You can use a simple rating system, such as assigning a number from 1 to 5 to each assignment based on its relevance. Prioritize the most important things first, and then move on to the less important items on your list.

- **Create a Schedule:**Making a schedule is another good time-saving method. Having a fixed schedule might help you remain on track and make better use of your time. Determine your most productive hours and schedule your most critical chores around them. Make sure to include breaks in your schedule to avoid burnout.

- **Use Time-Blocking:**Time-blocking is a popular time-saving technique that includes setting aside specified periods of time for specific tasks. For example, you may set aside 30 minutes to check and react to emails and another 30 minutes to make phone calls. You may boost your efficiency and get more done in less time by grouping comparable jobs together.

- **Minimize Distractions:**Distractions can be a significant time waster. To reduce distractions, turn off your phone, close your email inbox, and close any unneeded internet tabs. Consider wearing noise-canceling headphones to shut out background noise if you operate in a noisy area.

- **Delegate Tasks:**Delegating responsibilities can also be an efficient way to save time. Consider distributing responsibilities to team members or colleagues who can assist you with certain tasks. This will allow you to devote more time to more vital duties.

- **Use Technology to Your Advantage:**There are numerous time-saving solutions and technologies available to assist you in increasing your productivity. Project management software, for example, can help you keep organized and on track with your work, and time-tracking apps can help you better understand how you spend your time.

- **Take Care of Yourself:**Finally, it is critical to take care of yourself in order to maintain the energy and focus required for productivity. Get enough sleep, exercise frequently, and eat a balanced diet. Self-care will help you stay focused and productive throughout the day.

In conclusion, time-saving tactics can be a useful tool for anyone trying to boost their productivity and make better use of their time. You may increase your productivity and achieve your goals more efficiently by prioritizing your work, making a timetable, minimizing distractions, delegating tasks, utilizing technology, and taking care of yourself.

Chapter 7 Outsourcing and Delegation

Delegating and outsourcing chores might help you free up time to focus on your priorities. In this chapter, we'll go over the advantages of delegating and outsourcing, as well as how to execute them efficiently.

Effective time management is critical for success in any endeavor, whether personal or professional. Delegating and outsourcing tasks is one of the most effective strategies for managing your time. Delegating and outsourcing allow you to focus on what you do best while freeing up time and resources to focus on other elements of your life. In this chapter, we will look at the advantages of delegating and outsourcing, as well as some recommendations for doing so efficiently.

The Advantages of Delegation and Outsourcing

Delegating and outsourcing are important time management practices that can help you reach your objectives more effectively. Here are some of the advantages:

- **Time-Saving:**Delegating and outsourcing chores might help you save a lot of time. When you delegate responsibilities to others, you free up your time to focus on your key talents. Similarly, outsourcing jobs can save you time by allowing you to leverage the knowledge of others and focus on the tasks that are most important to you.

- **Increased Productivity:**Task delegation and outsourcing can boost your productivity. You may get more done in less time by focusing on your skills and outsourcing chores that you are not excellent at. This can help you attain your objectives more quickly and efficiently.

- **Improved Quality:**When you assign responsibilities to others, you can benefit from their knowledge and experience. This can help you improve the quality of your job and achieve greater outcomes.

- **Reduced Stress:**Task delegation and outsourcing can help to minimize stress. When you have too much on your plate, it is easy to feel overwhelmed and worried. You may lower your workload and stress levels by delegating responsibilities to others, enabling you to focus on what you do best.

Delegation and outsourcing strategies

- **Identify tasks that can be delegated:**Identifying the tasks that can be delegated is the first step in efficient delegation and outsourcing. Begin by generating a list of the duties you now undertake, then identify those that can be assigned to others.

- **Choose the right people:**When delegating and outsourcing jobs, it is critical to select the correct people. You must verify that the individuals you select have the essential abilities and knowledge to carry out the tasks efficiently.

- **Provide clear instructions:**It is critical to provide precise instructions when assigning responsibilities. This will help guarantee that the activity is completed appropriately and that no misunderstandings occur.

- **Set deadlines:**When delegating and outsourcing tasks, it is critical to establish timelines. This will help to ensure that the assignment is finished on time and without delays.

- **Monitor progress:**When delegating and outsourcing jobs, it is critical to monitor progress. This will help guarantee that the task remains on track and that no problems arise.

- **Provide feedback:**When delegating and outsourcing tasks, it is critical to provide feedback. This will assist the person carrying out the activity in understanding what they performed well and where they may improve.

- **Review and evaluate:**When the activity is over, it is critical to assess and evaluate the outcomes. This will assist you in identifying areas for improvement and ensuring that the assignment was completed satisfactorily.

Conclusion

Delegating and outsourcing are important time management practices that can help you reach your objectives more effectively. You can save time, enhance productivity, improve quality, and reduce stress by delegating responsibilities to others and outsourcing jobs that you are not excellent at. To delegate and outsource effectively, you must first identify the tasks that may be delegated, then select the appropriate personnel, issue clear instructions, set deadlines, monitor progress, provide feedback, and assess and analyze the results. You can efficiently delegate and outsource chores and achieve success in your personal and professional lives by following these recommendations.

Chapter 8 Distraction Control

Distractions can be a significant time waster, but they are also an unavoidable part of life. In this chapter, we'll look at typical distractions and ways to deal with them so you can stay focused and productive.

Distractions are a constant source of difficulty for those attempting to manage their time wisely. We are constantly distracted in today's society, from social media updates to email alerts to colleagues popping in for a conversation. If left unchecked, these distractions can have a negative impact on our productivity, making it difficult to complete tasks on time.

The capacity to manage distractions is required for effective time management. In this chapter, we'll look at several ways to reduce distractions and improve your time management skills.

- **Determine Your Distractions:**The first step in dealing with distractions is identifying what causes them. Consider what draws your focus away from work, such as social media, email, phone calls, or even others walking into your workstation. After you've recognized your distractions, you may work on developing tactics to reduce their impact.

- **Establish clear goals and priorities:**Setting clear goals and priorities is one of the most effective methods to manage distractions. It is simpler to stay focused and fight distractions when you know what you need to do in a day. Make a to-do list for the day and prioritize the most critical things first. This will assist you in remaining focused on the most critical duties and avoiding distractions from less important tasks.

- **Utilize Time-Blocking:**time-blocking is a technique that involves scheduling specified blocks of time for various tasks. This can assist you in staying concentrated and avoiding distractions from other tasks. For example, you may set aside time in the morning to check email, another for social media, and still another for finishing a certain assignment. You'll be less likely to be distracted by other things if you focus on one task at a time.

- **Disable notifications:**Notifications from social media, email, and other applications can be quite distracting. To reduce interruptions, consider turning off notifications during work hours. Set aside particular times to check your email or social media if you're concerned about missing critical communications. You can also use options like "Do Not Disturb" mode or "Focus" mode to reduce distractions at various times of the day.

- **Make Your Workspace Distract-Free:**A messy desk can be quite distracting. Take some time to organize your office and get rid of any clutter. Consider establishing a separate, distraction-free workspace. Close the door or use noise-canceling headphones if possible to reduce distractions from coworkers or outside sounds.

- **Take frequent breaks:**Regular breaks might help you maintain attention and avoid burnout. Schedule brief breaks throughout the day to allow yourself to rest and refocus. Consider taking a short stroll, doing deep breathing exercises, or a quick meditation during your breaks. When you return to work, this can help you clear your thoughts and increase your attention.

- **Maintain accountability:**Finally, keeping your goals and priorities in mind can help you manage distractions more efficiently. Share your objectives with a coworker or a friend and ask them to hold you accountable. Use a time-tracking app or tool to track your progress throughout the day. This might assist you in staying on course and avoiding distractions.

In conclusion, minimizing distractions is critical for good time management. You may reduce distractions and increase productivity by identifying your distractions, making clear goals, employing time-blocking, shutting off notifications, creating a distraction-free workspace, taking regular breaks, and staying accountable. You may gain the discipline and focus required to get more done in less time with practice.

Chapter 9 Continuous Evaluation and Improvement

Effective time management is a continual process that necessitates regular evaluation and development. In this last chapter, we'll go over how to assess your progress, find areas for development, and tweak your plans as needed to ensure long-term success.

Effective time management is a vital skill for personal and professional success. It enables people to prioritize tasks, accomplish them efficiently, and achieve their objectives. Time management, on the other hand, is not a one-time exercise; it takes ongoing work, assessment, and development to achieve long-term success. This chapter will go over the significance of reviewing and constantly developing time management abilities.

Examining time management abilities entails evaluating prior performance and identifying opportunities for development. This method can be repeated on a regular basis, such as weekly or monthly, to assess progress and make required changes. To begin, individuals should reflect on how they have spent their time, what tasks they have completed,, and which ones they have not. It is critical, to be honest and impartial during this process because it will aid in identifying flaws and areas for growth.

Individuals should discover areas for improvement after examining past performance. This could involve more effectively prioritizing activities, minimizing distractions, and enhancing productivity. The Eisenhower Matrix, which divides work into four categories: urgent and important, important but not urgent, urgent but not important, and not urgent and not important, is one method for prioritizing tasks. Individuals can use this matrix to prioritize their work based on priority and urgency.

Individuals can reduce distractions by using tactics such as time blocking, which involves scheduling specified blocks of time for specific work and minimizing interruptions during those blocks. It is also beneficial to avoid needless distractions during work hours, such as social media alerts. Setting attainable goals, breaking work down into smaller, manageable steps, and delegating jobs when appropriate can all help to increase productivity.

Continuous improvement entails making constant changes to time management abilities in order to maintain success. Individuals must evaluate their success on a regular basis and make appropriate improvements to their techniques. Setting explicit goals and benchmarks for improvement and tracking progress on a regular basis may be beneficial. Individuals will be able to recognize areas that need to be improved and change their tactics accordingly.

It should be noted that effective time management necessitates a commitment to ongoing development. It is a lifelong process rather than a one-time effort. Individuals may maximize their productivity, attain their goals, and live a more satisfying life by constantly reviewing and improving their time management abilities.

To summarise, efficient time management is a key skill that requires frequent evaluation and improvement. Individuals can improve their time management abilities and achieve their goals more efficiently by reflecting on prior performance, finding areas for growth, and making required adjustments. Individuals who are willing to spend time and effort improving their time management abilities will reap the advantages of higher productivity, enhanced performance, and a more rewarding life.

Chapter 10 Conclusion

Congratulations! You've completed "Time's Revolution: Take Control of Your Time to Transform Your Life." We hope that this book has given you useful ideas and practical solutions for better time management.

Effective time management is critical to attaining your objectives and having a satisfying life. You can take control of your time and accomplish more than you ever thought possible if you follow the principles and tactics taught in this book.

We've covered the essential ideas of time management throughout this book, such as the necessity of creating objectives, prioritizing activities, and being deliberate about how you spend your time. We've also given you a variety of tools and tactics for improving your time management abilities, from creating a daily routine to mastering the art of delegation.

However, we recognize that time management is not a one-size-fits-all solution. Everyone has different objectives, priorities, and circumstances, so what works for one person may not work for another. As a result, it's critical to try out different ways and see what works best for you.

We encourage you to continue prioritizing your time, being deliberate in your choices, and remaining flexible and adaptive in the face of changing circumstances as you move forward. Remember that good time management is about using your time in a way that supports your goals and allows you to live a fulfilling life, not about being busy for the sake of being busy.

We hope this book has been a useful resource for you as you strive for better time management. Thank you for reading it, and we wish you the best of luck in your future endeavors.